Superfairies

Farrah the Shy Fawn

by Janey Louise Jones
illustrated by Jennie Poh

PICTURE WINDOW BOOKS
a capstone imprint

Superfairies is published by Picture Window Books
A Capstone Imprint
1710 Roe Crest Drive
North Mankato, Minnesota 56003
www.mycapstone.com

Library of Congress Cataloging-in-Publication Data

Names: Jones, Janey, 1968- author. | Poh, Jennie, illustrator. | Jones, Janey,
1968- Superfairies.
Title: Farrah the shy fawn / by Janey Louise Jones ; illustrated by Jennie
Poh.
Description: North Mankato, Minnesota : Picture Window Books, a
Capstone imprint, [2016] | Series: Superfairies | Summary: It is the
beginning of summer and Farrah the fawn wants to look beautiful for the
petal parade, but when she tries the leaves of a supposedly magical plant
they just seem to make her sick, and the superfairies have to rescue her.
Identifiers: LCCN 2016007955| ISBN 9781515804321 (library
binding : alk. paper) | ISBN 9781515804345 (pbk. : alk. paper) | ISBN
9781515804369 (ebook pdf : alk. paper)
Subjects: LCSH: Fawns--Juvenile fiction. | Fairies--Juvenile fiction. |
Forest animals--Juvenile fiction. | CYAC: Deer--Fiction. | Fairies--Fiction. |
Forest animals--Fiction.
Classification: LCC PZ7.J72019 Far 2016 | DDC [E]--dc23
LC record available at http://lccn.loc.gov/2016007955

Designer: Alison Thiele

To our little princess Ella, love from Mummy and Daddy (Linda & Tony)
– Janey Louise Jones

For Kiana x
– Jennie Poh

Printed in China.
009694F16

Table of Contents

The Fairy World

The Superfairies of Peaseblossom Woods use
teamwork to rescue animals in trouble. They
bring together their special superskills,
petal power, and lots of love.

Superfairy Rose
can blow super healing fairy
kisses to make the animals in
Peaseblossom Woods feel better.

Superfairy Berry can see for miles around with her super eyesight.

Superfairy Star can create super dazzling brightness in one dainty spin to lighten up dark places.

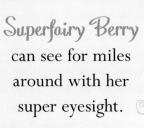

Superfairy Silk spins super strong webs for animal rescues.

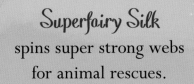

Chapter 1

Petals in the Woods

It was sunny and hot in Peaseblossom Woods.

Butterflies fluttered through the bright blue cornflowers and red poppies while the four Superfairies got ready to leave the cherry blossom tree.

"It's such fun wearing fresh flowers in our hair!" said Star.

"You look lovely!" said Rose with a smile. "But we must get going! I have the petals we collected yesterday here. Now, let's go scatter them!"

"Coming, Rose!" called Berry and Silk.

They flew out of the cherry blossom tree, up into the air and above the treetops. They began scattering flower petals on the path in the woodland below.

The petals floated down slowly, like perfumed pink raindrops. The air began to smell of petal perfume.

Farrah the Fawn was stepping through the woods daintily.

"Oh, what a lovely smell of flowers," she said.

Farrah saw the Superfairies at work.

"Hi, Farrah!" called Rose.

Farrah blushed shyly. "Hey, Superfairies, why are you scattering petals?" she called.

"We are marking the route for the Petal Parade," said Rose. "It will take place later today. Didn't you know? It always happens at the start of summer. The Petal Princess is coming!"

"Ooh, I forgot about the parade. I'm so excited," said Farrah.

"Well, we must keep on scattering," said Berry. "Goodbye, Farrah! See you later!"

"Bye!" called Farrah.

Farrah felt a little lonely now that the Superfairies had left. She went to tell her friend, Susie Squirrel, about the Petal Parade.

Susie *had* remembered about the Petal Parade. She was busy getting ready.

Farrah thought Susie looked lovely!

"Oh, your eyes look so sparkly," said Farrah.

"Thanks. I washed them with cucumber juice," explained Susie. "It brightens up tired eyes. Mom said so."

"Oh, and your cheeks are very rosy today!" said Farrah.

"I washed my face in the early morning dew," said Susie. "Granny said that was a good idea."

"Your fur is so shiny!" said Farrah.

"Ah, that's because I washed in rose water," said Susie. "Sorry I can't chat. I must polish my teeth with mint leaves. See you at the parade! Isn't it about time for you to get ready, Farrah?"

"Um, yes, I should, actually," agreed Farrah. But she had no idea what she was going to do to get ready.

Farrah's mom always said, "You are lovely just as you are." She didn't think beauty potions and perfumes were a good idea at all.

Mom will never let me try all that stuff. I'll never be as pretty as Susie, thought Farrah. *I wish I could look really beautiful for the parade!*

Farrah arrived back at her house. Mom was taking a nap.

Farrah had an idea.

I'll get ready all by myself and surprise Mom!

Farrah tried to remember all the things that Susie had used to make herself so sparkly and pretty.

Farrah decided to mix her very own beauty potion to make her look prettier.

She went into the kitchen.

First, she filled
a bowl with fresh
raspberry juice.
Oooh, juicy!

Farrah licked her hooves.

Next, she added lots
of honey. Oooh, sticky!

She took a little taste.
Yum!

Next, she poured
in sweet peach juice.
Oooh, messy!

Finally, she added
a handful of oats and
water. Oooh, gloopy!

Farrah stirred the mixture together with a twig and then spread it over her cheeks and legs.

At first it felt warm. Then it felt tight. Next, it was a little itchy. And then it became horribly itchy!

"Ughhhh!" she cried as the mixture dried on her coat in sticky lumps.

"I'll need to go and wash this off in the pond. I don't think this is going to make me look pretty at all!"

Chapter 2

The Rainbow Plant

The pond wasn't far away. Mr. Frog was perched on his favorite lily pad.

"Hello, Mr. Frog!" called Farrah, jumping into the water.

"Hello, little one. Are you feeling the heat?" asked Mr. Frog.

"Yes, it's very hot, but I'm also itchy, actually," said Farrah.

As she splashed the mixture off her coat with the cool, fresh water, Farrah saw her reflection in the pond and sighed sadly.

"What's the matter?" asked Mr. Frog.

"Oh, it's just that I want to be pretty for the parade," she said. "Can you help me?"

"Well, I think you're already lovely, just as nature made you," said Mr. Frog. "But if you want to try a beauty treatment, why not use the leaves from the Rainbow Plant?"

"What's that?" asked Farrah.

"I've heard it's a plant that grows higher up on Rainshine Hill," said Mr. Frog. "They say one flower head has petals of every color of the rainbow. Apparently, it can make you beautiful! But I don't know if it's true . . ."

"I'll try it!" said Farrah. "That sounds like a great idea. The Rainbow Plant! It even sounds pretty!"

"Just follow the river upstream, and you will see Rainshine Hill. I believe the Rainbow Plant is about halfway up there."

"Thanks, Mr. Frog.
I'll see you at the
Petal Parade later on."

Off Farrah went
in search of the
Rainbow Plant.

She skipped
along the
riverbank . . .

. . . did
cartwheels
through
Buttercup
Meadow . . .

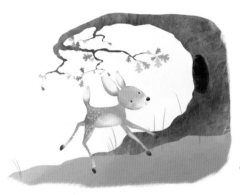

. . . cantered past Orlando Owl's house . . .

. . . and danced right up Rainshine Hill to the Rainbow Plant!

"Phew, I'm so hot!" said Farrah.

The petals were like the smoothest silk—and just as Mr. Frog had said, they were every color of the rainbow.

Farrah took some of the petals and began to rub them on her cheeks and legs.

Oh, please make me as pretty as Susie, she thought.

Farrah was exhausted after finding the plant. She decided to lie down in the sunshine for a few minutes.

Back at the cherry blossom tree, the Superfairies finished laying out the picnic blankets. They were for the party that would take place after the Petal Parade.

Wildflowers grew around the tree and large bowls of strawberries were placed on the cloths. There were jugs of freshly made lemonade and honey loaves, too.

"Time to make petal crowns for our friends for the parade!" announced Rose, carrying a basket of freshly picked wildflowers.

The Superfairies gathered around and chose blooms from the basket. They got busy making the crowns.

Just as Rose was about to place her crown on her head, the Superfairies heard the bells ringing. Softly at first. Then stronger.

They got louder and louder.

Ting-aling-aling . . .

Ting-aling-aling . . .

The Superfairies forgot all about their flower crowns. The safety of the animals was the most important thing to them.

"Oh dear!" said Berry. "Someone's in trouble!"

"Prepare to rescue!" said Rose.

"Who's in danger?" asked Silk.

Rose checked the Strawberry computer.

"It's little Farrah the Fawn!"

"Where is she?" asked Berry.

"She's near Orlando Owl's house, not far from Rainshine Hill," said Rose.

"What's happened to her?" asked Silk.

"I can't see exactly. But she's not walking well, and she looks tired, dizzy, and confused," said Rose. "Orlando Owl rang the bells as soon as he saw her."

"Oh, poor little Farrah," said Star. "I wonder what the problem could be. Let's get to her as quickly as we can!"

The Superfairies jumped into the fairycopter and went through their rescue checklist as quickly as possible.

"Everything's in order," said Berry.

She always flew the fairycopter because of her super eyesight. She looked up ahead as she planned her route. "We'll follow the riverbank from above."

"Prepare to rescue!" said Rose. "5, 4, 3, 2, 1 . . . go, go, go!"

The Superfairies flew over the woods in their fairycopter with Berry at the controls.

Chapter 3

Farrah in Trouble

Farrah made her way shakily down the side of Rainshine Hill. Orlando Owl flew overhead, feeling very worried about her.

"Are you okay, Farrah?" he asked. "I rang the bells for the Superfairies."

"Oh dear," she said. "What's happened to me? I don't feel well at all."

"What have you been doing?" said Orlando. "Can you think of anything that might have made you feel sick? Why are you so far out of the woods?"

Farrah thought that the leaves of the Rainbow Plant might have made her feel miserable. She wanted to explain everything to Orlando Owl, who was always helpful and sensible. But she couldn't get the words out right. Farrah was all mixed up!

"Rainbow leaves from the Rainbow Plant . . . Mr. Frog . . . Petal Parade . . . Susie so pretty . . . need the Superfairies," she chattered on, making no sense at all.

Oh dear, poor little thing. She thinks there's something called a Rainbow Plant! thought Orlando.

Farrah was so dizzy that she had to rest against a tree.

Berry and the other Superfairies were up above in the fairycopter.

On the woodland floor below, they could see Farrah's mom looking around anxiously. She had obviously realized that Farrah was missing.

"Thank goodness she seems to be heading in the right direction," said Rose. "We can let her know what's happening as soon as we land."

"I'm looking for a space to land," said Berry. "Does the Strawberry say where Farrah is now?"

Rose checked the computer.

"She was resting by a tree at the bottom of Rainshine Hill, but she's staggering back into the woods now. Near Orlando Owl's house," explained Rose.

"Okay, I'll get as near to Orlando's house as possible," said Berry.

"Let's get everything ready," said Rose. "I don't know why she's so dizzy. She needs us right away."

Orlando Owl tried to tell Farrah to settle in one spot until the Superfairies arrived, but she wouldn't listen to his advice.

Farrah saw some beautiful scented flowers growing behind a cluster of trees.

"I can hear a stream. I'm so thirsty," she said.

Orlando followed, feeling worried that the Superfairies would never find them now.

Farrah walked through the cluster of trees and saw an archway of summer flowers up ahead. The sound of water was louder and stronger.

It looked as if the archway of flowers led to a secret place . . .

Farrah was curious.

Orlando Owl fluttered above her, looking over his shoulder to see if the Superfairies were there yet.

Farrah stepped closer to the flowery arch.

She could see petals floating in the summer breeze. She could smell sweet perfume. She could hear the tinkling water.

Hop!

Before she knew it, Farrah was on the other side of the archway.

She saw a fabulous flowery fairy glade, with a stream of pure, clear water running through the middle.

What was this beautiful place?

The home of the Petal Princess! At the center was a fairy throne, and all around were flowers, birds, butterflies, bumblebees, and curious enchanted trees.

"Wow!" said Farrah.

She trotted farther into the flowery den.

Chapter 4

The Petal Parade

Farrah followed a path to the stream and noticed the Petal Princess looking at herself in the water. The princess was quite unaware that she had visitors— Farrah the Fawn and Orlando Owl were so quiet.

"A few flowers in my hair will look nice for the parade," said the princess.

She suddenly noticed Farrah.

"Oh, hello, little fawn," the Petal Princess said. "Are you all right?"

"Um, no, I'm not, actually," said Farrah.

"What happened?" asked the Petal Princess kindly.

"I don't know exactly. I was trying to look pretty for the parade this afternoon," said Farrah. "And I heard about the Rainbow Plant . . . May I have a drink of water?"

"Of course," said the Petal Princess. "This is all very confusing!"

"I rang the bell for the Superfairies," said Orlando. "I've been following her since I noticed her staggering down the hill. But I'm afraid to say she's making no sense at all."

Farrah drank from the clear, cool stream.

"I needed that," she said.

And with that, she fell to the floor as if she were fast asleep.

"Poor little thing!" said the Princess. "The Rainbow Plant does no good at all. It's a silly myth."

"You mean the leaves *don't* make you beautiful?" said Orlando.

"No, nothing can make you beautiful except the goodness in your own heart," explained the Petal Princess.

Just then, there was a fluttering of wings.

The Superfairies arrived at the woodland home of the Petal Princess.

"Hello, Petal Princess!" they cried.

"Oh, thank goodness!" said the princess. "How did you know to come here?"

"Our Strawberry computer led us here," said Rose.

"Just in time!" said the Petal Princess. "Farrah is very sick indeed."

"Let's look at you, Farrah," said Rose, examining the little fawn, who was still half asleep. "Poor little deer. Berry has gone to get her mom—they've been searching for her in the woods."

"She's had a drink of water," said the Petal Princess. "Whatever can be wrong?"

Rose examined Farrah for a few moments.

"It's most probably sunstroke!" said Rose. "Farrah has been out in the hot sun for too long."

"Rose, you are brilliant," said Star. "I'd never have thought of that. What should we give her?"

"Ah, lots of water, rest, and some healing kisses will do the trick!"

Rose blew gentle kisses onto Farrah's hot little forehead.

"Oh, that's better already!" Farrah said with a smile, waking up from her sleep. At that moment, her mom arrived with Berry.

Farrah nuzzled her mother happily!

"Now," said Star. "How can we keep Farrah out of the strong sun at the parade?"

"I think I can help with that!" said the Petal Princess.

She went away for a few moments and came back with a petal parasol for Farrah.

"I will hold you in my arms as I fly through the woods during the parade. This parasol will shield us both from the sun," said the Petal Princess.

Farrah beamed with pride.

"Thank you!" she exclaimed. "I can't believe it. Susie will be so excited for me!"

Later that afternoon, Farrah overcame her shyness as she flew at the head of the Petal Parade. She was delighted to be with the Petal Princess and the Superfairies.

"Hey, you look lovely!" called Susie.

"And so do you!" called Farrah.

Farrah had never felt so happy and proud.

It was time for the picnic back at the cherry blossom tree.

As the older animals enjoyed the delicious strawberries, the Petal Princess played games with the little animals.

"Let's play In and Out the Dusting Bluebells!" said Farrah, full of energy again.

"Thank you for taking care of her, Superfairies. You saved her life!" said Farrah's mom.

"Orlando Owl and the Petal Princess did that," said Rose with a smile.

The Superfairies were relieved that everyone in the woods was safe and happy again. It was time for their song!

Fairies from the blossom tree,
Superskills galore have we.

Caring in this charming wood
For needy animals, as we should.

Twinkle, sparkle, dazzle, swish,
Tending animals as they wish.

And when a rescue's nicely done,
It's time to have some fairy fun.

Dancing, singing, twirling, glee,
All around our blossom tree!

Glossary

arch (ARCH)—the curve above a doorway or opening

dew (DOO)—tiny drops of water that form at night

myth (MITH)—an old story, often magical

parasol (PAR-uh-sawl)—a light umbrella used to give shade from the sun

perfume (PUR-fyoom)—a pleasant smelling liquid to dab on the body

potion (POH-shuhn)—a liquid with magical powers

reflection (re-FLEK-shuhn)—the image you can see in a surface like a mirror

secret (SEE-krit)—something unseen by others

staggering (STAG-uh-ring)—walking or moving unsteadily

Talk It Out

1. Talk about a picnic you have enjoyed in sunshine. Where did you go? What did you eat? What did you play? Were you careful in the sunshine?

2. Do you think it is more important to look nice or to be nice?

3. Why is it always best to tell your parents where you are going? How does Farrah get in trouble when she doesn't do this?

Write It Down

1. Write a thank you letter to the Superfairies from Farrah the Fawn.

2. Draw a picture of the sun. Draw a line down the middle of it. On one side, write about nice things to do in sunshine. On the other, write about ways you must be careful in the sun.

All About Fairies

The legend of fairies is as old as time. Fairy tales tell stories of fairy magic. According to legend, fairies are so small and delicate, and fly so fast, that they might actually be all around us, but just very hard to see. Fairies, supposedly, only reveal themselves to believers.

Fairies often dance in circles at sunrise and sunset. They love to play in woodlands among wildflowers. If you sing gently to them, they may very well appear.

Here are some of the world's most famous fairies:

The Flower Fairies

Artist Cicely Mary Barker painted a range of pretty flower fairies and published eight volumes of flower fairy art from 1923. The link between fairies and flowers is very strong.

The Tooth Fairy

She visits us during the night to leave money when we lose our baby teeth. Although it is very hard to catch sight of her, children are always happy when she visits.

Fake Fairies

In 1917, cousins Elsie Wright and Frances Griffiths said they photographed fairies in their garden. They later admitted that most were fakes—but Frances claimed that one was genuine.

Which
Animal Friend Are You?

1. In a picnic, what is most important?
   - A) sandwiches
   - B) cakes
   - C) fruit
   - D) cheese

2. What kind of dancing sounds like the most fun?
   - A) ballet
   - B) ballroom
   - C) tap
   - D) disco

3. What color parasol would you like best?
   - A) white
   - B) purple
   - C) pink
   - D) blue

4. Which perfume smell would you pick?
   - A) honeysuckle
   - B) violets
   - C) roses
   - D) lemons

5. If you are really thirsty, what do you like to drink?
   - A) water
   - B) milkshake
   - C) lemonade
   - D) orange juice

6. If you had to wear a fancy hat, what would it be covered in?
   A) white flowers
   B) purple flowers
   C) pink flowers
   D) mud

7. What's the first thing you would pack for a day out?
   A) a book to read
   B) bat and ball
   C) bubble blower
   D) football

8. On a sunny day, do you:
   A) quietly think about what to do
   B) run outside and go wherever it's sunniest
   C) see what your friends want to do
   D) charge off on an adventure, forgetting your sunscreen!

Mostly A—you are like Farrah Fawn. You are sweet, lovable, and a bit shy at times.

Mostly B—you are like Violet Rabbit. You are fun-loving and enjoy new things. You make a great friend.

Mostly C—you are like Susie Squirrel. You are thoughtful and kind, but you like to play as well!

Mostly D—you are like Basil Bear. You enjoy exploring new things. You love company and lots of laughs.

About the Author

Janey Louise Jones has been a published author for 10 years. Her *Princess Poppy* series is an international bestselling brand, with books translated into 10 languages, including Hebrew and Mandarin. Janey is a graduate of Edinburgh University and lives in Edinburgh, Scotland with her three sons. She loves fairies, princesses, beaches, and woodlands.

About the Illustrator

Jennie Poh was born in England and grew up in Malaysia (in the jungle). At the age of 10 she moved back to England and trained as a ballet dancer. She studied fine art at Surrey Institute of Art & Design as well as fashion illustration at Central Saint Martins. Jennie loves the countryside, animals, tea, and reading. She lives in Woking, England with her husband and two wonderful daughters.

JOIN THE
SuperFairies
ON MORE
MAGICAL
ANIMAL RESCUES!

Basil the Bear Cub
by Janey Louise Jones

Dancer the Wild Pony
by Janey Louise Jones

Martha the Little Mouse
by Janey Louise Jones

Violet the Velvet Rabbit
by Janey Louise Jones

Sonny the Daring Squirrel
by Janey Louise Jones

Farrah the Shy Fawn
by Janey Louise Jones

THE Fun DOESN'T STOP HERE!